That's What a Friend Is

WRITTEN AND ILLUSTRATED

BY P.K. HALLINAN

Ideals Children's Books • Nashville, Tennessee

Published by Ideals Children's Books
An imprint of Hambleton-Hill Publishing, Inc.
Nashville, Tennessee 37218

Printed and bound in the United States of America

ISBN 0-8249-8492-7

A friend is a listener who'll always be there

when you've got a big secret you just have to share.

A friend is a sidekick
who'll sit by your side

to make you feel better
when you're troubled inside.

And when there's nothing to do on a wet rainy day,

a friend is a pal who'll come over to play.

Friends are just perfect
for all kinds of things,

like walking...
or talking ...

or swinging on swings!

And for watching TV,
a friend is the best

for cheering cartoons
with,
and booing the rest.

And then late at night
a friend is just right

for telling ghost stories
when you've turned off
the light.

Yes, a friend is the best
one
to hop, skip, or run with...

You can sing and shout 'til your tonsils wear out,

'cause that's what having a friend's all about!

A friend is a buddy
who'll come to your aid

when he thinks you need
help,
or you might be afraid.

A friend is a partner who'll stand back to back to protect you from bullies, or a monster attack.

With a friend you can do
what you most like to do!

You can have your own
hideouts

in dark, secret places...

or spend the whole day
having caterpillar races

or just drawing pictures
of each other's faces.

You can laugh...

you can cry...

you can watch cars
go by...

you can have a great time
and not even try!

A friend is a person
who likes to be there...

'cause you two
make a wonderful pair!

And when all's said and done,
the natural end is ...

a friend is a friend...
THAT'S what a friend is!